This book belongs to
my friend:

_____

Problem solving

Published by Scholastic Inc., 90 Old Sherman Turnpike, Danbury, CT 06816.

SCHOLASTIC and associated logos are trademarks and/or registered trademarks of Scholastic Inc.

ISBN 0-7172-7794-1

Printed in the U.S.A.

First Scholastic Printing, March 2007

Dora's Nursery Rhyme Adventure

by
Christine Ricci

illustrated by
Jason Fruchter

SCHOLASTIC INC.

New York   Toronto   London   Auckland   Sydney
Mexico City   New Delhi   Hong Kong   Buenos Aires

"Jack and Jill went up the hill
To fetch a pail of water . . ."

Dora was reading her baby brother and sister their favorite nursery rhyme. The babies snuggled up next to their big sister.

Suddenly Dora and the twins saw a big rain cloud pass over Jack and Jill's hill. The storm blew Jack and Jill down the hill!

After the cloud blew away, Dora and the twins noticed that Jack and Jill had tumbled far from their hill.

"Help!" cried Jack and Jill. "We've got to get back to our hill!"

"We need to use our story powers to help Jack and Jill," exclaimed Dora. "Are you ready for a storybook adventure?"
The babies nodded excitedly. Then Dora and the twins held hands and jumped into the book.

Dora and the twins landed right next to Jack and Jill.
"We can help you get back to your hill," said Dora.
"But our hill is very far away," Jack told her.
"And we don't know how to get there," added Jill.

"Our friend Map can tell us how to get there," Dora told them.
Map popped out of Backpack's pocket. "First you
have to go past Humpty Dumpty, then go past Old
King Cole's castle. And that's how you'll get to
Jack and Jill's hill," Map told them.

"So first we have to find Humpty Dumpty," Dora said.

"*¿Dónde está?* Where is Humpty Dumpty?"

The babies pointed to Humpty Dumpty in the distance.

"I'm lost," cried Humpty Dumpty when they reached him. "I got turned around during the storm. Where do I usually sit?"

"We'll help you," said Dora. She started to sing. "*Humpty Dumpty sat on a . . .*"

"Wall!" exclaimed the twins.

As Humpty Dumpty climbed to the top of his wall,
the babies sang the rest of the nursery rhyme:
"Humpty Dumpty had a great fall;
All the King's horses and all the King's men
Couldn't put Humpty together again!"

"Oh no!" cried Dora. "Humpty Dumpty might get hurt. Does Backpack have anything to cushion his fall?"

"Pillows!" exclaimed the babies.

The babies, Jack and Jill, and Dora made a soft
landing spot next to the wall.

"*¡Gracias!*" said Humpty. "Now I'll be safe."

"*De nada*," Dora replied. "Next we have to find
Old King Cole's castle. Which path should we take?"

"I see the castle," said Humpty Dumpty.
"Just follow the green path."
"Thanks, Humpty!" Jack and Jill called.

17

When everyone arrived at Old King Cole's castle, they peeked inside the open door. Much to their surprise, the castle was a mess!

"Looks like the rain cloud came through here, too," Jack observed.

Just then they heard someone crying in the next room. "C'mon!" urged Dora. "It sounds like Old King Cole needs our help!"

The King was sad because he couldn't find the things that made him happy.

"We need to figure out what makes him happy," Dora said. She and the babies started to sing:

"Old King Cole was a merry old soul,
And a merry old soul was he.
He called for his pipe,
He called for his bowl,
And he called for his fiddlers three."

"Great!" Dora exclaimed. "We need to find a pipe, a bowl, and three fiddlers."

21

Dora, the twins, and Jack and Jill found everything that made the King happy.

"Thanks for helping me," Old King Cole said merrily. "Now how can I help you?"

"Can you help us find our hill?" asked Jack and Jill.

The King took everyone to the top of the castle's highest tower.

"I see lots of hills," said Dora. "Which one is Jack and Jill's hill?"

"Our hill has a well on the top of it so we can fetch a pail of water," Jack told them.

"Ah yes," said the King. "There is your hill."

But when they reached the top of Jack and Jill's hill, the rain cloud suddenly appeared again.

"We know what to do," said Dora. She and the twins sang, "*Rain, rain, go away; Come again another day.*"

"I don't like that nursery rhyme!" puffed the rain cloud, and it blew far, far away.

"Hooray!" everyone cheered.

Jack and Jill gave Dora and the babies a big hug.

After saying good-bye to Jack and Jill, Dora and the babies jumped out of the book and landed back in the twins' room. Soon the babies were sound asleep.

"Well, that was quite a nursery rhyme adventure," Dora whispered, as she kissed them goodnight. "We did it! *¡Lo hicimos!*"

Nick Jr. Play-to-Learn™ Fundamentals
Skills every child needs, in stories every child will love!

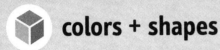 **colors + shapes**
Recognizing and identifying basic shapes and colors in the context of a story.

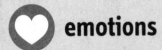 **emotions**
Learning to identify and understand a wide range of emotions, such as happy, sad, and excited.

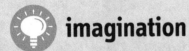 **imagination**
Fostering creative thinking skills through role-play and make-believe.

 **math**
Recognizing early math in the world around us, such as patterns, shapes, numbers, and sequences.

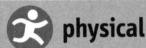 **music + movement**
Celebrating the sounds and rhythms of music and dance.

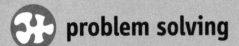 **physical**
Building coordination and confidence through physical activity and play.

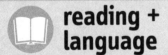 **problem solving**
Using critical thinking skills, such as observing, listening, and following directions, to make predictions and solve problems.

 **reading + language**
Developing a lifelong love of reading through high interest stories and characters.

science
Fostering curiosity and an interest in the natural world around us.

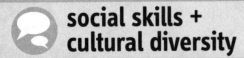 **social skills + cultural diversity**
Developing respect for others as unique, interesting people.

Problem Solving

Conversation Spark

Questions and activities for play-to-learn parenting.

Dora, the twins, and Jack and Jill helped Humpty Dumpty by putting pillows under his wall. What would you do to help?

For more parent and kid-friendly activities, go to www.nickjr.com.

ENGLISH/SPANISH GLOSSARY and PRONUNCIATION GUIDE

English	Spanish	Pronunciation
Where is	Dónde está	DOHN-day eh-STAH
Thank you	Gracias	GRAH-see-ahs
You're welcome	De nada	deh NAH-dah
We did it	Lo hicimos	loh ee-SEE-mohs